LITTLE MISS
CHATTERBOX

by Roger Hargreaves

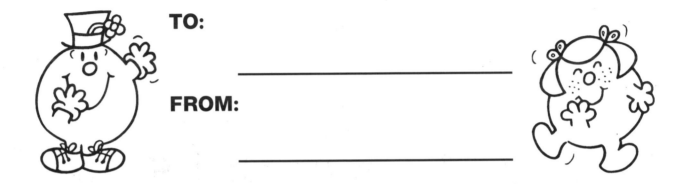

TO: _____

FROM: _____

EAN

ISBN 978-0-8431-9889-8

9 780843 198898

5 0 4 9 9

little Miss Chatterbox

by Roger Hargreaves

PSS!

PRICE STERN SLOAN

An Imprint of Penguin Group (USA) Inc.

Little Miss Chatterbox talked more than a lot.

She talked all the time.

Day in and day out, week after week, month after month, year in and year out!

She never stopped!

She didn't know it, but she even talked in her sleep!

She had a brother.

I bet you can guess what his name was!

Can't you?

That's right!

Mr. Chatterbox!

She looks a bit like him, don't you think?

You should have heard them when they got together!

You couldn't get a word in edgeways.

Or sideways.

Or anyways!

Have you ever heard about somebody being able to talk the hind leg off a donkey?

Well, Mr. Chatterbox could talk both hind legs off a donkey.

And his sister could talk the hind leg off an elephant!

Now, this story is about the time Little Miss Chatterbox decided to get herself a job.

Which she did.

In a bank.

In Happyland.

At ten o'clock one Monday morning, Mr. Happy strolled into the HappyToLendYouBank in the middle of Happytown.

He took out his checkbook, wrote a check, and went to the counter.

Behind the counter, on her first morning at work, stood Little Miss Chatterbox.

She smiled at Mr. Happy.

Mr. Happy smiled back.

"Good morning," he said, cheerfully.

"Well," said Little Miss Chatterbox, taking a deep breath . . .

"For the time of the year it is a good morning but not as good as the morning we had yesterday and I dare say tomorrow morning will be an even better morning but it's quite a good morning for a Monday morning and . . ."

And she went on and on and on until it was time for the bank to close.

Mr. Happy was still standing there, with his mouth open in amazement.

He'd been there for hours!

"And now," continued Little Miss Chatterbox, "it's time for the bank to close and time for me to go home so good-bye and nice talking to you and . . ."

And she went home, leaving poor Mr. Happy without any money.

The following morning she was fired!

She got herself another job.

In a restaurant.

The Eatalot!

It was Tuesday, and at noon Mr. Greedy walked into the restaurant and sat himself down at his usual corner table.

He always ate there on Tuesdays because that was the day they served extra large portions.

The waitress came up to take his order.

"What's the soup of the day?" Mr. Greedy asked the waitress.

"Well," said Little Miss Chatterbox—for she was the waitress—"the soup of the day is tomato but we also have other soups on the menu such as oxtail and vegetable and chicken and chicken noodle but we have lots of other things to start with such as . . ."

And she went on and on and on.

Until midnight!

Mr. Greedy was still sitting there, listening in amazement.

He'd been there for twelve hours!

Listening!

"And now," continued Little Miss Chatterbox, "it's time for the Eatalot Restaurant to close and for me to go home so good-bye and nice talking to you and . . ."

And she went home, leaving poor Mr. Greedy feeling rather empty.

The next morning she was fired!

The same thing happened all week long.

On Thursday morning she was fired from her job as an assistant in a hat shop.

Miss Splendid went into the shop to buy herself a new hat, but she couldn't!

"Oh Madam I've just the hat for you and I know you're going to love it because it's pink and pink is your color and it . . ."

It was all talk and no hat!

On Friday morning she was fired from her job as a secretary to Mr. Uppity.

Mr. Uppity, incidentally, was the richest man in the world!

I just thought you'd like to know.

But poor Mr. Uppity didn't make any money the day that Little Miss Chatterbox was working for him.

Oh, no!

"Oh Mr. Uppity I've never worked in an office before and isn't it exciting and would you like a cup of coffee and are you as rich as everybody says you are and it . . ."

It was all talk and no work!

But this story has a happy ending, because at the very end of that week Little Miss Chatterbox managed to find herself a job that suited her down to the ground.

And up to the sky!

That Saturday evening Mr. Chatterbox was at home in Chatterbox Cottage.

Which was where he lived.

Mr. Chatterbox was mad because his watch had stopped and he had arranged to meet Little Miss Sunshine at seven o'clock and he had no idea what the time was.

So he decided to call the Time to find out what time it was.

He dialed the number.

". . . at the tone the time will be six twenty-five and fifteen seconds!"

Little Miss Chatterbox took a deep breath.

BEEP!

"At the tone the time will be six twenty-five and twenty seconds!"

BEEP!

"That's funny," thought Mr. Chatterbox to himself. "That sounds just like my sister!"

www.ilovemrmen.com

ISBN 978-0-8431-9889-8   10 9 8 7 6 5 4 3 2

MR. MEN   LITTLE MISS

PRICE STERN SLOAN

Little Miss Bossy

 Little Miss Naughty

 Little Miss Neat

 Little Miss Sunshine

 Little Miss Tiny

 Little Miss Trouble

 Little Miss Giggles

 Little Miss Helpful

 Little Miss Magic

 Little Miss Shy

 Little Miss Splendid

 Little Miss Twins

 Little Miss Chatterbox

 Little Miss Ditzy

 Little Miss Late

 Little Miss Lucky

 Little Miss Scatterbrain

 Little Miss Star

 Little Miss Busy

 Little Miss Quick

 Little Miss Wise

 Little Miss Tidy

 Little Miss Greedy

 Little Miss Fickle

 Little Miss Brainy

 Little Miss Stubborn

 Little Miss Curious

 Little Miss Fun

 Little Miss Contrary

 Little Miss Somersault

 Little Miss Scary

 Little Miss Bad

 Little Miss Whoops

$4.99 US
($5.99 CAN)

ISBN 978-0-8431-9889-8

PSS!
PRICE STERN SLOAN
www.penguin.com/youngreader

EAN

9 780843 198898

5 0 4 9 9

...ricans

MARTIN LUTHER KING, JR.

CIVIL RIGHTS LEADER

Patricia and Fredrick McKissack

Enslow Elementary
an imprint of
Enslow Publishers, Inc.
40 Industrial Road
Box 398
Berkeley Heights, NJ 07922
USA
http://www.enslow.com

For Ruth Ness and Richard Petway

Enslow Elementary, an imprint of Enslow Publishers, Inc.

Enslow Elementary® is a registered trademark of Enslow Publishers, Inc.

Original edition published as *Martin Luther King, Jr.: Man of Peace* © 1991.

Library of Congress Cataloging-in-Publication Data

McKissack, Pat, 1944–
  Martin Luther King, Jr. : civil rights leader / Patricia and Fredrick McKissack.
    p. cm. — (Famous African Americans)
  Includes bibliographical references and index.
  Summary: "A simple biography about Martin Luther King, Jr. for early readers"—Provided by publisher.
  ISBN 978-0-7660-4099-1
  1. King, Martin Luther, Jr., 1929-1968—Juvenile literature. 2. African American civil rights workers—Biography—Juvenile literature. 3. African Americans—Civil rights—History—20th century—Juvenile literature. I. McKissack, Fredrick. II. Title.
  E185.97.K5M358 2012
  323.092—dc23
  [B]
                              2012013435

Future editions
Paperback ISBN 978-1-4644-0203-6
ePUB ISBN 978-1-4645-1116-5
PDF ISBN 978-1-4646-1116-2

Printed in the United States of America

082012 Lake Book Manufacturing, Inc., Melrose Park, IL

10 9 8 7 6 5 4 3 2 1

To Our Readers: We have done our best to make sure all Internet Addresses in this book were active and appropriate when we went to press. However, the author and the publisher have no control over and assume no liability for the material available on those Internet sites or on other Web sites they may link to. Any comments or suggestions can be sent by e-mail to comments@enslow.com or to the address on the back cover.

Every effort has been made to locate all copyright holders of material used in this book. If any errors or omissions have occurred, corrections will be made in future editions of this book.

♻ Enslow Publishers, Inc., is committed to printing our books on recycled paper. The paper in every book contains 10% to 30% post-consumer waste (PCW). The cover board on the outside of each book contains 100% PCW. Our goal is to do our part to help young people and the environment too!

Photo Credits: AP Images, pp. 10, 20; AP Images/Chick Harrity, pp. 1, 4; AP Images/Gene Herrick, p. 13; Library of Congress, p. 3.

Illustration Credits: Ned O., p. 7, 8, 14, 16.

Cover Illustrations: AP Images/Chick Harrity

Words in bold type are are explained in Words to Know on page 22.

Series Consultant:
Russell Adams, PhD
Emeritus Professor
Afro-American Studies
Howard University

CONTENTS

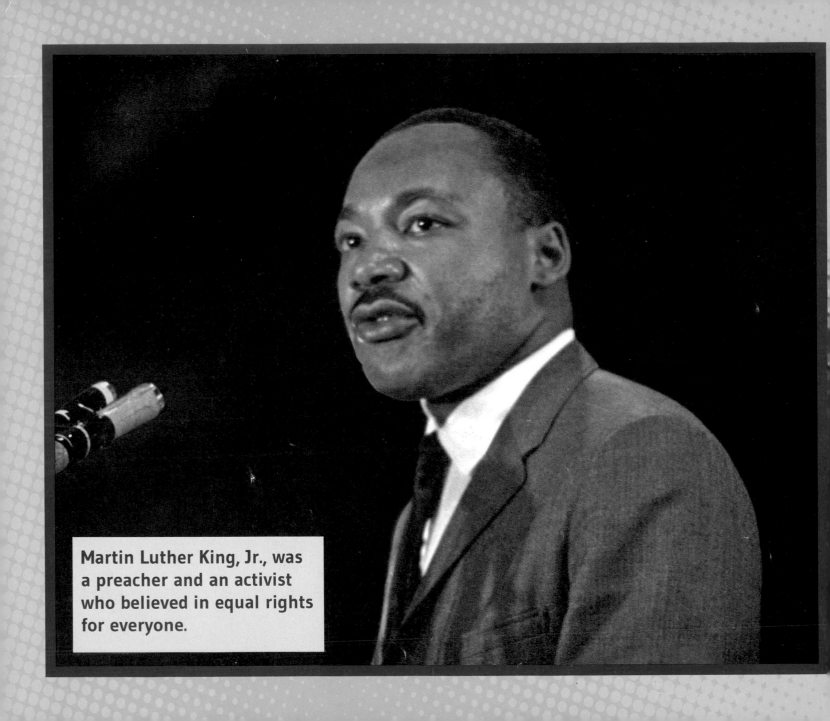

Martin Luther King, Jr., was a preacher and an activist who believed in equal rights for everyone.

CHAPTER 1
BECAUSE YOU ARE COLORED

Martin Luther King, Jr., was born on January 15, 1929. He grew up in a big house on Auburn Avenue in Atlanta, Georgia.

Martin Luther King, Sr., was a Baptist **preacher**. Everybody called him Daddy King. He was a strong, proud man who taught his children to be proud also. Alberta King was "Mother Dear" to her three children.

Young Martin's family called him M.L. But his friends called him "**Tweed**," because he wore tweed suits. His friends also called him "Will Shoot," because whenever the basketball was passed to him, he would shoot it.

There was also a serious side to Martin. He questioned **segregation**. Segregation meant that black people were treated differently from other people. Why did they have to ride on the back seats of buses? Use separate public bathrooms? And drink from different water fountains? Martin was told: Because you are **colored**!

That's the way things were in the South when Martin was growing up. Once, Martin made a speech and won first place. He and his teacher rode the bus home. The bus filled up. So the driver told all the black riders that they had to give up their seats to white passengers. When Martin asked why, he was told: Because you are colored!

Even though Martin Luther King, Jr., was young, he felt segregation was not a good way for Americans to live. Black and white people should have the same rights.

Growing up in the South, Martin and other black people were not treated the same as white people.

Dr. Benjamin Mays became Martin's close friend. Dr. Mays helped Martin decide what he wanted to do with his life.

CHAPTER 2
MOREHOUSE AND MORE . . .

Martin still had fun growing up. He loved the good **soul-food** meals prepared by his grandmother. He did so well in school that he graduated from high school when he was only fifteen. In the fall of 1944, he entered Morehouse College in Atlanta.

What was Martin going to be? Daddy King said he should be a preacher. Martin wasn't so sure about that. He was still very young. He had a lot of questions about people, God, and what he would do in life.

A very important person in his life during that time was Dr. Benjamin Mays, the **president** of Morehouse. Dr. Mays was a very good friend and helped Martin look for his own answers.

By the time he finished Morehouse in the class of 1948, Martin knew he wanted to be a preacher. So he went to Crozer Theological **Seminary** in Chester, Pennsylvania.

Martin Luther King, Jr., third from left, sits at an assembly at Morehouse College in 1948.

At Crozer, Martin read about Mohandas Gandhi, who helped India gain freedom from England—peacefully. Martin also read the writings of Henry David Thoreau, who said unfair laws should not be obeyed. Martin studied the words of Jesus and other holy leaders. His studies helped him find ways to fight **prejudice** peacefully.

There was racial prejudice in the North as well as in the South. But whenever it came up, Martin handled it peacefully. His classmates looked up to him, and even his enemies became his friends.

Love and peace were becoming very important words in Martin Luther King, Jr.'s life.

CHAPTER 3
PEACEFUL PROTEST

After finishing Crozer Seminary in 1951, Martin went to Boston University. While living in Boston, Martin met Coretta Scott from Alabama. She was studying music at a school in Boston.

After their first date, Martin asked Coretta to marry him. She thought he was joking, but he wasn't. "She was everything I wanted in a wife," he told his best friend. And on June 18, 1953, Martin and Coretta were married.

Martin got his advanced degree in **theology**, and Coretta finished her studies, too. Then the Kings had to decide where they would live. A church in the South had asked Dr. King to come there. Mrs. King wanted to stay in the North at first. The South was still very segregated. But at last, they decided to go back "down home."

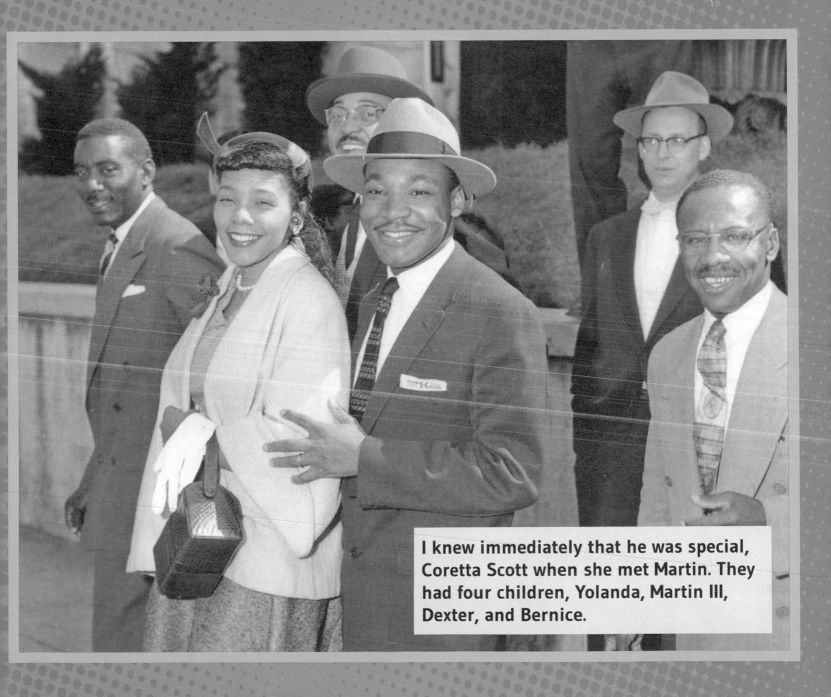

I knew immediately that he was special, Coretta Scott when she met Martin. They had four children, Yolanda, Martin III, Dexter, and Bernice.

Dr. King led a peaceful bus strike in Alabama. The protest worked! Black riders would have the same rights as white riders.

In December 1954, the Reverend Dr. Martin Luther King, Jr., preached his first sermon as the pastor of Dexter Avenue Baptist Church in Montgomery, Alabama.

A year passed. It was December 1, 1955. An African-American woman named Rosa Parks got off from work and boarded a public bus. The bus filled, so she was asked to give up her seat to a white passenger. Mrs. Parks refused. At that time, it was against the law for Mrs. Parks to refuse to give up her seat to a white person when the bus was crowded. So she was taken to the police station.

Black leaders in Montgomery called a meeting that evening at Dr. King's church. It was decided that a bus strike might help to change the unfair laws. Dr. King was asked to be the leader. He said he would, but only if the people taking part in the bus strike were peaceful.

For months and months, black people of Montgomery didn't ride the public buses. One year later, the bus company agreed to let all people, black and white, sit where they wanted.

In the 1960s, students held sit-ins at lunch counters. Often they were called names and had things thrown on them.

CHAPTER 4
TO THE MOUNTAINTOP

· ·

After the Montgomery bus strike, Dr. King started the Southern Christian Leadership Conference (SCLC). He moved his family to Atlanta. Daddy King was very happy to have his son and family home again.

The South was changing. Young people were helping it happen. **Students** at North Carolina A&T University held peaceful **sit-ins** at segregated lunch counters.

Black and white students were working together to make America a better place. They formed a group under the SCLC known as the Student **Non-Violent** Coordinating Committee, or SNCC (pronounced "snick"). The group held sit-ins and peaceful protests all over the country. Americans were taking a stand against segregation—even if it meant they were beaten or put in jail. Dr. King was jailed many times, too.

But he always said to stay peaceful.

In 1963, two well-known leaders, A. Philip Randolph and Bayard Rustin, planned the March on Washington for Jobs and Freedom. Other black leaders were asked to take part.

On a hot August morning in 1963, more than 250,000 people came to Washington, D.C., to the largest **demonstration** for rights ever held in this country! People came from all over the world in airplanes, trains, buses, and cars. Some walked, and some were carried. The large crowd was orderly and peaceful. They sang songs. A favorite was called "We Shall Overcome."

Many people gave speeches that day. At the end of the long day, there was one more speaker: Martin Luther King, Jr.

He talked about having a dream where Americans lived in peace and friendship. "Let freedom ring," he said. And one day, he hoped all Americans might sing, "Free at last, free at last. . . ."

CHAPTER 5
WE SHALL OVERCOME

For his work, Dr. King was given the **Nobel Peace Prize** in 1964. He was the second African American to win this high honor.

President John F. Kennedy had pushed for laws that would protect the rights of all races. But he had been killed on November 22, 1963. President Lyndon B. Johnson wanted to work for equal rights, too. Dr. King was at the White House the day President Johnson signed the Voting Rights Act on August 6, 1965.

Dr. King believed in peace. Some people didn't. They beat his followers. Churches were burned. Dogs and water hoses were turned on peaceful marchers. People were put in jail. Some were even killed. Many times people said they wanted to kill Dr. King.

In his most famous speech, Dr. King spoke about his hope that someday all people could live in peace. He spent his life working toward that dream.

Workers in Memphis, Tennessee, asked him to help them plan a peaceful march. Dr. King went to Memphis.

The march ended in **violence**. This bothered Dr. King very much. He wanted to hold another march. So he returned to Memphis.

He stayed at the Lorraine Motel. On April 4, 1968, Martin Luther King, Jr., was killed by James Earl Ray. Ray served a life sentence in a Tennessee state prison. He died in 1998.

Mrs. Coretta King began the Center for Non-Violent Social Change, in Atlanta. People come from all over the world to study Dr. King's life, writings, and peaceful demonstrations.

Today the birthday of Martin Luther King, Jr., is a holiday. Every year, on the third Monday in January, we honor his work and his dream. If his dream is remembered, then one day we might live together in peace.

Words to Know

colored—An outdated name for African Americans.

demonstration—A public showing of feeling for or against an issue.

Nobel Peace Prize—A special honor given to a person who works for peace in the world.

nonviolent—Peaceful, without violence.

preacher—A teacher of religion.

prejudice—Dislike of people, places, or things without a good reason.

president—The leader of a country or group.

segregation—Keeping people apart from one another because of race, religion, age, sex, or some other reason.

seminary—A school where religion is studied.

sit-in—A kind of demonstration; at the first sit-ins, blacks and whites sat at whites-only lunch counters waiting to be served. Later, sit-ins were used to object to different things, like war, poverty, and world hunger.

soul-food—Food made popular by African Americans in the South.

students—People who attend school.

theology—The study of religion.

tweed—A warm, heavy material made of different colors of wool woven together.

violence—Acts that hurt or destroy people, places, animals, and other things.

Learn More

Books

King, Jr., Martin Luther. *I Have a Dream.* New York: Scholastic, 2007.

Mara, Will. *Martin Luther King, Jr.* New York: Children's Press, 2003.

Rappaport, Doreen. *Martin's Big Words: The Life of Dr. Martin Luther King, Jr.* New York: Hyperion Books, 2007.

Web Sites

Martin Luther King Jr. Online
<http://www.mlkonline.net/home.html>

The King Center
<http://www.thekingcenter.org>

"Martin Luther King, Jr."
<http://seattletimes.nwsource.com/mlk>

Index